my many emotions

Fear

I0877205

Cherry Lake Press

Published in the United States of America by Cherry Lake Publishing Group
Ann Arbor, Michigan
www.cherrylakepublishing.com

Reading Adviser: Beth Walker Gambro, MS, Ed., Reading Consultant, Yorkville, IL
Content Adviser: Emily Fragapane, M.Ed., Ed.S., Nationally Certified School Psychologist, RYT200
Book Designer: Jennifer Wahi
Illustrator: Jeff Bane

Photo Credits: © Kleber Cordeiro/Shutterstock.com, 5; © jwblinn/Shutterstock.com, 7; © Shane N. Cotee/Shutterstock.com, 9; © Prostock-studio/Shutterstock.com, 11; © Alexander_Safonov/Shutterstock.com, 13; © MAD_Production/Shutterstock.com, 15; © TY Lim/Shutterstock.com, 17; © Mariia Kalinichenko/Shutterstock.com, 19; © fizkes/Shutterstock.com, 21; © Yuganov Konstantin/Shutterstock.com, 23; Cover, 2-3, 6, 14, 22, 24, Jeff Bane

Copyright © 2022 by Cherry Lake Publishing Group
All rights reserved. No part of this book may be reproduced or utilized in any form or by any means without written permission from the publisher.

Cherry Lake Press is an imprint of Cherry Lake Publishing Group.

Library of Congress Cataloging-in-Publication Data

Names: Devera, Czeena, author. | Bane, Jeff, 1957- illustrator.
Title: Fear / by Czeena Devera ; illustrated by Jeff Bane.
Description: Ann Arbor, Michigan : Cherry Lake Publishing, [2021] | Series: My many emotions | Includes index. | Audience: Grades K-1
Identifiers: LCCN 2021004885 (print) | LCCN 2021004886 (ebook) | ISBN 9781534186958 (hardcover) | ISBN 9781534188358 (paperback) | ISBN 9781534189751 (pdf) | ISBN 9781534191150 (ebook)
Subjects: LCSH: Fear--Juvenile literature. | Emotional intelligence--Juvenile literature. | Social learning--Juvenile literature.
Classification: LCC BF575.F2 D49 2021 (print) | LCC BF575.F2 (ebook) | DDC 152.4/6--dc23
LC record available at https://lccn.loc.gov/2021004885
LC ebook record available at https://lccn.loc.gov/2021004886

Printed in the United States of America
Corporate Graphics

table of contents

About the author: Czeena Devera grew up in the red-hot heat of Arizona surrounded by books. Her childhood bedroom had built-in bookshelves that were always full. She now lives in Michigan with an even bigger library of books.

About the illustrator: Jeff Bane and his two business partners own a studio along the American River in Folsom, California, home of the 1849 Gold Rush. When Jeff's not sketching or illustrating for clients, he's either swimming or kayaking in the river to relax.

Have you ever felt an **uneasiness** you can't explain? Maybe you feel like your feet need to be under the covers. Or you double-check the closet before bed. That's **Fear**.

How would you describe Fear?

Fear can come suddenly. It feels like a shock.

Is that a spider on the wall? Eek!

Fear is a normal **reaction**. Your body is trying to protect you. It can be helpful.

Feeling Fear around strange dogs can keep you safe. Not all dogs are nice!

Sometimes, it's fun to be scared. Watching scary movies is fun because it's just **pretend**.

But it’s not fun when you let Fear control you. Sometimes, it stops you from trying new things.

How does Fear feel to you?

Fear can make your mouth feel dry. It can make your hands sweaty.

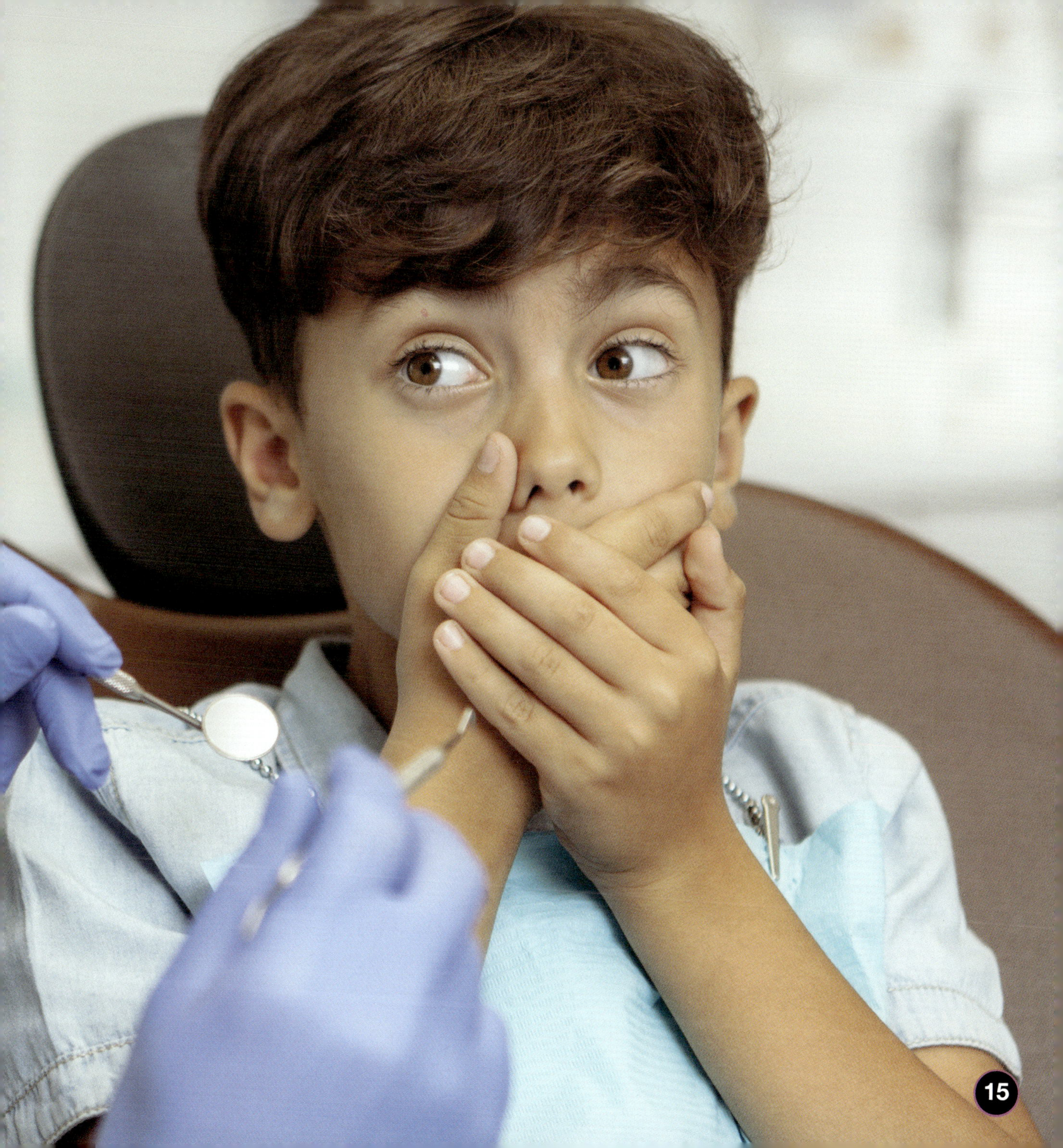

Fear might make you want to run. Or it can make you freeze up. You might feel stuck in place.

Take a moment to pause. Make a list. Think of the thing that scares you. Write down what to do if it happens. Making a plan can help you feel safe.

Sometimes, Fear can make you feel **helpless**. But you're not. Ask for help. Talk to a trusted adult.

How do you
show Fear?

Remember, it's okay to feel Fear.
You are stronger than you think.

glossary & index

glossary

fear (FIHR) the state of being afraid

helpless (HELP-liss) without support or protection

pretend (pri-TEND) not real

reaction (ree-AK-shuhn) a behavior or response to something

uneasiness (uhn-EE-zee-nuhss) a feeling of discomfort

index